ESPECIALLY FOR GIRLS®

ESPECIALLY FOR GIRLS® Presents

Once Upon a Dark November

CAROL BEACH YORK

Holiday House / New York

This book is a presentation of **Especially for Girls®**,
Newfield Publications, Inc. Newfield Publications offers
book clubs for children from preschool through high school.
For further information write to: **Newfield Publications, Inc.**,
4343 Equity Drive, Columbus, Ohio 43228.

Published by arrangement with Holiday House.
Especially for Girls and Newfield Publications are
federally registered trademarks of Newfield Publications, Inc.

First Edition

Library of Congress Cataloging-in-Publication Data

York, Carol Beach
Once upon a dark November/by Carol Beach York.—1st ed.
p. cm.
Summary: A high school freshman with a crush on her English
teacher, Katie enjoys her job doing housework in his house until a
murder in his family has Katie fearing for her own life.
ISBN 0-8234-0780-2
[1. Mystery and detective stories.] I. Title.
PZ7.Y820n 1989
[Fic]—dc19 89-2021 CIP AC
ISBN 0-8234-0780-2

Prologue

No breath of air stirred in the dense green heat of the summer afternoon. Flowers drooped along the side of the white frame house and a heavy silence hung over Linden Street.

The next nearest house was at the corner, half a block away.

Bees droned over meadow flowers in the tall grass—and at the white frame house the muffled sounds of screaming and kicking in the attic closet finally stopped.

In the dining room a woman sat with a newspaper spread open on the table: *The Granville News*. Lunch dishes had long ago been cleared from the table, and the lace cloth was bare except for the open newspaper. Potted ferns stood beside dining-room windows that gave a view of the side yard and high sunlight.

The woman nodded to herself as she read bits of local news. *Methodist Church potluck supper Saturday night . . . Mr. and Mrs. William Simpson announce the engagement of their daughter . . . Fourth of July parade on Freemont Street . . .*

At last, when she thought enough time had passed for even the naughtiest child to learn a lesson, the woman closed up the newspaper and went through the house to the front stairway. The banister was dark with varnish, the way up shadowed at this time of day. At the landing a small round window was like the curtained porthole of a ship sailing in the shadows.

When the woman reached the second floor, she stood for a moment at the foot of the narrow, steeper steps to the attic. All around her there was only the silence of the house.

"Auntie's coming, dear," she called sweetly.

She grasped the stair rail to help herself up, since she was a heavy woman and felt her weight.

"Auntie's coming."

The heat in the attic was overwhelming. All afternoon the sun had been beating on the roof. Dust specks glimmered in streaks of light at the windows.

When the closet door was unlocked, the face of the child peering from the dark was startling. A face pale and stunned, hovering there in the gloom of the closet.

"Now, now—no need to look like that." The woman was taken aback for a moment, even she. "Come along," she said, pulling at the child. "It was only Auntie's little joke. But we mustn't be naughty anymore, must we?"

Chapter One

In thirty-five years the town of Granville changed in some ways and remained the same in some ways.

The Methodist Church still had potluck suppers, but the suppers were in a new building now, a fine new church building with a taller spire and a larger choir loft.

New stores opened on Center Avenue, and then closed, as business gradually went to the shopping mall at the edge of town.

The population grew from 12,306 to 27,820. There were three new elementary schools and an addition to the high school that was larger than the original building.

Homes sprang up where vacant meadows had been, until the blocks were solid, house beside house. Television antennas rose from the roofs.

* * *

What remained the same was the statue of Abraham Lincoln in the town square.

The Granville News still reported church doings, weddings, and Fourth of July parades.

The tree-lined streets were still quiet.

Linden Street had been the same as long as Katie Allen could remember.

An only child, Katie had lived all of her fourteen years on Linden Street, in a red brick house shaded by evergreens and tall lilac bushes. She was a small girl with brown hair that fuzzed up on rainy days and a nose that freckled in the summer sun. She had a pet canary named Binky, and a best friend named Heather. Everyone along Linden Street knew Katie and would wave to her as she came by.

But November was beginning now and everybody was indoors. Katie hurried along on her way home from school, shivering a little in the cold air. Soon it would be time for boots and woolly scarves. Soon it would snow.

But before snowfalls came and true winter began, there were the dark days of November, marked at one end by Halloween and the other end by Thanksgiving. Between those two holidays Katie didn't think much of interest was likely to happen. November was dreary and bleak; the trees looked forlorn and bare; every afternoon it was dark by four-thirty.

On this first day of November, Halloween was not yet completely gone. Jack-o'-lanterns still stood in front windows and on porch rails, grinning into the drab afternoon. A thin mist shrouded the top branches of the trees, fallen leaves rustled along the curb. Only the trick-or-treaters had been out the night before. Memories flooded back to Katie as she thought of her own trick-or-treat nights—full of excitement and thrilling fright when she was six, seven, eight years old.

Mr. McIvor's house had been the scariest place on those Halloween nights when Katie scurried around the neighborhood with her little friends. It took a dare to get anyone to run up Mr. McIvor's porch steps and ring his doorbell. He had no treats to give, so ringing his doorbell was just to give him a fright—if anybody took the dare. He had a mean dog chained in the yard, barking and straining at the chain to break free and spring upon small ghosts and goblins.

Mr. McIvor was dead and gone now, but Katie remembered.

Another place Katie had not liked to go was Miss Gorley's house, although it was not at all the same as Mr. McIvor's. Miss Gorley had treats to give, and she had no mean dog in her yard. Still, Katie hadn't liked going there.

There was something unpleasant about Miss Gorley that Katie couldn't exactly explain. Even as a little girl, Katie would hold tighter to her mother's hand if she saw Miss Gorley on the street. She hoped Miss Gorley wouldn't see her, but Miss Gorley always did. She would come close and bend down toward Katie. "How is the little girl today? Such a pretty little girl." Katie's mother would look pleased, but Katie didn't like Miss Gorley's face coming down close to hers, the rouged and powdered cheeks, the staring eyes.

On Halloween nights Miss Gorley came to the door, bending to peer into the masked faces of the children at her door. "Hello, dearies," she would say, smiling ever so sweetly. "Here're your candies." In the dim region beyond, Katie could glimpse a dark hall carpet and the banister of a stairway, bathed in pale light.

"Here're your candies, dearies—hold up your bags, that's the way—" the old voice would croon as the children crowded together at the open door. There was nothing to be afraid of, of course, but Katie had held out her trick-or-treat bag and looked up into that face with a fast-beating heart. And she ran away at once, as soon as the bit of candy had been dropped into her bag. Her only feeling of real safety came from knowing her own house was so close, just across the street.

Now Katie looked over at Miss Gorley's house as she walked along, coming home from school this November afternoon. The house stood against the autumn sky, framed by bare trees and low gray clouds. A single light burned in a downstairs window. Once white, the house was now weathered and gray, a towering old house, the oldest on the block, with three stories and tall windows where the curtains were drawn so no one could see in.

Miss Gorley didn't go out often now, being quite elderly. Katie's father usually shoveled her walk after a snowfall and Katie would see Miss Gorley watching at her living-room window. Occasionally Katie saw her on her porch or in her yard, and sometimes Katie's mother sent Katie over with something for Miss Gorley: a plate of cookies, a bowl of homemade potato salad. "Poor woman, all alone," Katie's mother said. And when Katie went over with whatever her mother was sending, it was like those long-ago Halloween nights . . . the door opening and the crooning voice, "Thank you, dearie—so kind of your mother—you're such a pretty girl—so kind to a poor old woman" . . . and beyond the door Katie could see the dark carpet and the curve of the banister at the stairway.

Katie had never been farther than the door.

Chapter Two

In contrast to Miss Gorley's house, Katie's house had a more cheerful aspect. Lights glowed in the windows; sturdy red and golden marigolds were still blooming in the front yard; a neighbor's car was in the driveway, with a HUG SOMEBODY TODAY bumper sticker. The kitchen door was unlocked and Katie let herself in, to a house filled with the smell of baking bread. Her mother worked part-time in a gift shop at the mall, but this was one of her days off.

"Hi, Mom . . . hi, Mrs. Lawson."

The kitchen table was cluttered with coffee cups, cookies, and the visiting neighbor's knitting. In his cage by the windows, Binky was preening his feathers.

"Hi, honey." Katie's mother turned toward the door as Katie came in. Mrs. Lawson looked up from a knitting magazine she was consulting. "Hello, beautiful. How's school?"

"Okay." Katie shrugged. She put her schoolbooks on the counter and with puckered lips made kissing sounds to Binky through the bars of the cage. A handful of cookies, and it was time to go. . . .

"See you later, Mom . . . Bye, Mrs. Lawson."

Now the fun part of Katie's day was beginning, and she hurried off happily—and hopefully—to her after-school job. At the corner she turned down Bell Street, toward the Herron house.

Two afternoons a week, Tuesday and Friday, Katie worked for Mrs. Herron. She dusted furniture, polished silver, sometimes ran errands, carried laundry down to the washer and dryer in the basement—whatever else Mrs. Herron wanted done. Mrs. Herron was a particular housekeeper. All her closets were in order. Everything in the downstairs bathroom was blue. Everything in the upstairs bathroom was green. A bowl of wax fruit sat on the exact center of the dining-room buffet. This week Mrs. Herron had told Katie she would be putting fresh shelf paper in the kitchen cupboards.

As Katie hurried along to Mrs. Herron's, the November gloom closed around her again. She felt the chill in the air more sharply. All the yards looked gray in the growing dusk.

Then ahead Katie saw the lights of the Herron house.

Would Mr. Herron be home?

She was always hopeful he would be.

Mr. Herron taught English at Granville High School. Katie had a crush on him, and she always felt a secret thrill when she was in his house. He was often at home, so she could really *see* him. If he wasn't home, there was the possibility that he might come at any moment. It made the job very suspenseful.

"How can you like *him*?" Katie's girlfriend Heather had been surprised to hear about this crush. Heather was a good-natured girl with yellow hair and blue eyes. Because she was Katie's best friend, she was the only one in whom Katie ever confided. Heather promised never, never to tell anyone, but she didn't understand why Katie liked Mr. Herron.

"He's probably as old as your father," Heather argued. "His hair is getting gray."

Katie had no answer. Crushes couldn't always be properly explained. They just happened. Katie had had a crush on Mr. Herron from the first day of school in September when he had walked into the freshman English class, fifth period, Room 104. It was a warm day, a warm, golden September day. The classroom windows were open and sunlight lay along the sills like a memory of summer. Mr. Herron came in just as the bell rang. He stood by his desk at the front of the room, waiting a moment for the class to give him its attention. He was not unusually handsome, and his hair was graying a bit at the temples—as Heather said;

but something about him caught Katie's fancy. "Good afternoon," he said, "my name is Mr. Herron."

Perhaps it was because Katie was there so close, in the first seat of the second row, that he began with her.

"You must help me get to know your names," he said, smiling as he gestured toward Katie.

"Katie Allen," she said, flushing. It always sounded so odd to say your own name; it was sort of embarrassing.

"Well, Katie, tell me who are some of your favorite authors."

Frantically Katie tried to think of her favorite authors. She liked to read, but no names came to mind. It was as though she had never read a book.

The classroom was silent.

"I have a lot of favorite authors," Katie said in desperation.

At the back of the room someone laughed and Mr. Herron's attention shifted from Katie for a moment. Then he looked back at her and winked an eye. "I have a lot of favorite authors too, Katie. I'm glad to know we have so much in common."

Ever since then, Katie had been dividing her time in English class between classwork and admiring Mr. Herron sitting at his desk, writing assignments on the blackboard, walking down an aisle or over to a window. Fifth period English was her favorite of all her classes.

* * *

On this November afternoon, Mr. Herron didn't seem to be home. Mrs. Herron opened the back door for Katie, and Katie could see fresh rolls of shelf paper on the kitchen counter.

Mrs. Herron was a thin, dark-eyed woman, as neat and tidy as her house. "You forgot your gloves," she noticed at once. She shook her head to show she believed teenagers were likely to do careless things like that.

Katie put her jacket on a kitchen chair and rubbed her hands to get them warm. It was nice to get in out of the darkening afternoon, out of the cold. She was used to Mrs. Herron, who seemed a nice enough woman even though she was a fussy housekeeper. "The more money for you," Heather was always reminding Katie. "You wouldn't have your job if she let everything get in a big sloppy mess. Then she wouldn't care."

It was impossible to imagine Mrs. Herron letting everything get in a big sloppy mess.

"I was just doing something in the basement." Mrs. Herron beckoned Katie to follow her down the stairs that led from the kitchen to the basement. "I have some things to put away from a party last night."

Katie followed her down the stairs covered with green linoleum, as Mrs. Herron talked:

"We went to a Halloween party last night with some of the faculty. I was just getting our costumes packed away."

In the basement a long fluorescent bulb shone down

on the washer and dryer. Above a tool bench a few tools hung on a pegboard—although John Herron, English teacher, was not handy with tools and owned only the basic ones. Lawn chairs were stacked firmly in a corner. On a laundry table by the washing machine the party costumes had been dumped in a heap, which was not Mrs. Herron's usually tidy way.

"What did you wear?" Katie went toward the costumes with interest. Mrs. Herron, fortyish, quiet, reserved, did not seem the type to dress up and go gliding off to a Halloween party. It was hard for Katie to picture her in the pale, silky dress that hung over the edge of the laundry table. Mrs. Herron always wore tailored blouses and cardigan sweaters and small pearl earrings. Her clothes were very uninteresting.

"I was supposed to be Juliet." Mrs. Herron made a face to show how ridiculous she thought this was. "John's idea, of course. He was Romeo. What else can we expect from an English teacher? Anyway, now I just want to get it all packed away."

"Did you wear this?" Katie was entranced with a small silver eye mask that lay on top of the costumes, and she fingered the material of the Juliet dress. "I bet you looked beautiful."

Mrs. Herron shook her head. "I'm sure I only looked foolish." Businesslike, she began to fold the Romeo costume, and Katie gathered up the silky dress . . . anybody would look beautiful wearing that, she thought.

''Miss Fenning was the one who looked beautiful,'' Mrs. Herron added, as though she knew she was giving out news that everybody already had.

Katie felt embarrassed, and a little sorry for Mrs. Herron. Miss Fenning was the Spanish teacher at Granville High, and she *was* very pretty. She wore violet eye shadow and dangling earrings, and lots of unusual Indian jewelry she had gotten on summer vacations to Mexico. There were no cardigan sweaters or small pearl earrings in Miss Fenning's closets—and her closets probably weren't as organized as Mrs. Herron's.

An old brassbound trunk stood by the tool bench, and as Mrs. Herron lifted the lid, Katie could see other masks and party costumes that had been collected through the years—a neatly folded red cape for a devil, a mysterious shiny black coat, shawls, fans, a pair of red shoes for the devil, a Frankenstein-monster mask with a tear in the chin.

In went the Juliet dress, Romeo's doublet and tights, the silver eye mask. Down came the lid of the trunk as Mrs. Herron gave an unconcealed sigh of relief. ''That nonsense is over for another year.'' She met Katie's solemn look and smiled bleakly. ''John is the one who likes dressing up, not me. But I always have to go along. I try to be a good sport.'' She made it sound like a sacred duty, agreed upon along with other marriage vows.

''Now let's see if we can get this trunk over in that corner.'' Mrs. Herron nodded toward a storage corner on the other side of the tool bench. And at just that moment Katie was overjoyed to hear footsteps in the kitchen above, and Mr. Herron's voice, "Hello—anybody home?"

"We're down here," Mrs. Herron called up the stairs. "You're just in time. Can you come and put this costume trunk away for me—it's too heavy for us."

Mr. Herron came down the basement stairs, still wearing his coat, and a white silk scarf, which Katie thought was very stylish.

"Hello there, Katie."

"Hello, Mr. Herron."

"I want you to put this trunk over there in that corner—" Mrs. Herron was busy with her instructions. "And while you're at it, you may as well pull out the Christmas boxes and put the trunk behind. Leave the Christmas stuff in front where I can get at it when the time comes. Which won't be long now."

Katie watched with admiration as Mr. Herron brought from the storage corner several large cardboard boxes labeled in red crayon: CHRISTMAS. With ease he shoved the cumbersome trunk back against the wall, then stacked the Christmas boxes into place in front of it. Costumes, masks, disguises, all the mystery and fun of Halloween done with and packed away for another year. The trunk disappeared from sight behind a wall of boxes of ornaments and tinsel, wreaths with artificial holly and berries, figures for a manger scene, strings of colored lights. Would Mrs. Herron's Christmas lights be tangled? Katie wondered. At Katie's house, strings of Christmas lights always were, no matter how carefully they had been put away the year before. They tried her father's patience every time.

"How's that?" Mr. Herron asked, when the boxes were in place. His scarf had slipped askew, which made him only more dashing in Katie's eyes. Never mind that Heather thought he was too old. Having a crush on Mr. Herron was like having a crush on a TV or movie star. In the real world, so to speak, Katie liked Donny Cramer best. He was just her age (no gray hairs on Donny's head), and he sat across the aisle in Spanish class. Sometimes after class he walked Katie down the hall to her algebra class.

"Our next job, Katie, is upstairs," Mrs. Herron said, giving a nod of approval toward the stacked boxes.

To Katie's regret, Mr. Herron lingered behind in the basement and she had no choice but to leave him there, handsome in his tan coat and white scarf, hardly noticing that she was going.

"I've just had a letter from a cousin of mine. I haven't seen him in years. It was quite a surprise to hear from him." Mrs. Herron talked over her shoulder to Katie as they went up the basement stairs, then up more stairs to the bedrooms on the second floor.

Katie wondered about the kitchen shelf paper, but apparently the cousin came first.

"Martin hasn't been in Granville for—oh, it must be twenty years, maybe more." Mrs. Herron's voice had a weary sound. "He hardly ever writes. Now he wants to come for a visit. Well, what can you do when it's a relative? You have to let him come.''

They had reached the second floor. From a central hall, carpeted in tasteful beige, Mrs. Herron's favorite color, doors opened to the bedrooms and to Mr. Herron's study. Mrs. Herron stepped into one of the bedrooms. ''I want to get this guest room ready for Martin,'' she said. ''He's coming tomorrow. I suppose the bed first.''

The large bed by the windows had only a spread over it, so they made it up with fresh sheets.

''A blanket from the linen closet,'' Mrs. Herron directed, and Katie went out into the hallway to get the blanket. Maybe Mr. Herron would come upstairs just at the moment she was there in the hallway by the linen closet.

He didn't.

Katie went slowly, stalling for time. She took a blanket—slowly—and then put it back and took another—slowly— Any second Mr. Herron might appear at the head of the stairs . . . he did not appear.

Finally Katie carried her blanket back to the guest room.

''There are plenty of hangers in the closet,'' Mrs. Herron was musing to herself as she surveyed the guest room to see what else she might do. A carafe and water glass stood on the bedside table, ready for use. There were magazines on the table. Everything looked fine to Katie.

Beyond the curtains that parted at the windows Katie could see the November twilight drawing in. Mrs. Herron turned on the bedside lamp, and for a moment the room basked in a cozy light. Then unexpectedly Mrs. Herron drew her arms around herself as if she were cold. More to herself than to Katie she said, "No good will come of this visit—that's one thing I know." There was an almost fearful note in her voice.

Katie stood by the bed, startled. Mrs. Herron had forgotten her; she stood staring at nothing; Katie could have been a million miles away. The small beam of lamplight wasn't enough to shut out the growing darkness beyond the windows.

Something bad was going to happen. Katie felt that quite certainly. Standing there in the room with Mrs. Herron, Katie felt an apprehension that was more than just the gloomy spell of the dark November day. Something bad was going to happen . . . sometime soon . . . when Cousin Martin came.

Chapter Three

As the week went on the weather turned unseasonably warm. Fog drifted over the streets. As Katie walked home from school, houses in the distance ahead vanished into the mist.

On Thursday she was later than usual and it was nearly dark as she came home. The fog lit the streets like a ghostly vapor. She was late because she had gone to the library with Heather. There, while the misty air pressed against the library windows, Katie and Heather sat close together writing their reports for American history: "The West Conquered."

Some older girls they recognized from school came in, one of them jingling car keys, and Heather nudged Katie. "That's us in a couple of years."

They watched the girls from lowered eyes.

"I want a coat exactly like that," Katie whispered, as the girl with the car keys unbuttoned a red wool coat.

When the girls had gone to their own study table, "The West Conquered" was still waiting for Katie and Heather.

As they left the library, going their separate ways, Katie took the long way home—to Bell Street and past the Herron house. Mr. Herron would surely be home from the high school by now. Perhaps he would be out in his yard raking the last of the fallen leaves, or just coming out to get in his car for some errand or other. Sometimes she had been lucky that way. And on this afternoon, she thought she was lucky again. Mr. Herron was just coming around the side of the house with Mrs. Herron, walking toward the car that was in the driveway. Then, after a moment of joy at her good fortune, Katie saw that the man walking beside Mrs. Herron wasn't Mr. Herron after all. It was a man she had never seen before and could not even now see very well in the gloom and mist of the late afternoon. She could see eyeglasses and a mustache, enough to know it wasn't Mr. Herron . . . and then she realized it must be Mrs. Herron's cousin, who hardly ever wrote letters and now had invited himself for a visit. A visit Mrs. Herron had a bad feeling about.

Mrs. Herron and her cousin didn't notice Katie going by, and she hurried past, glancing back as she neared the corner. Mrs. Herron and her cousin were getting into the car. As Katie turned the corner she could see the headlights go on, flooding the bushes by the garage with light. Mr. Herron, alas, was nowhere in sight.

That was Katie's first sight of Cousin Martin.

When she went to the Herron house the next day for her regular Friday afternoon, he was sitting at the kitchen table drinking a cup of coffee. It startled her to see him sitting there, where no one had ever been sitting when she came.

Mrs. Herron, opening the door for Katie, was ready with introductions.

"Martin, this is Katie, my little helper. She comes after school on Tuesdays and Fridays."

The man at the table looked at Katie without interest.

"Katie, this is my cousin Martin." Mrs. Herron continued the introductions with her impeccable good manners.

"Hello," Katie said, feeling shy.

Cousin Martin nodded briefly. Light shone on his eyeglasses. *No good will come of this visit,* Mrs. Herron had said.

"So you have a helper these days, Laura," Cousin Martin said thoughtfully. "Things are going well for you."

"Well enough, I suppose." Mrs. Herron unrolled shelf paper on the kitchen counter and measured with a ruler. "I couldn't get along without Katie," she said; Cousin Martin nodded, stirring sugar into his coffee.

Katie felt uncomfortable as she unzipped her jacket. She wished Cousin Martin would go somewhere else in the house. Why didn't he go up to the nice guest room Mrs. Herron had fixed for him?

"You can use the step stool, Katie," Mrs. Herron said. She wanted to get right on with the shelf papering, which had only been partly done on Katie's previous afternoon. There was nothing for Katie to do but pull the step stool over to the cupboards, although she felt self-conscious having to work right under Cousin Martin's eyes. She was all thumbs, nervous that she might drop the cups and saucers she was handing down to Mrs. Herron, or perhaps fall off the step stool altogether. How embarrassing that would be!

Occasionally she peeked at Cousin Martin as she handed down something from the shelves. He reminded her of an owl, blinking behind the round, rather thick glasses. He didn't seem interested in what she was doing, to her relief—or interested in what Mrs. Herron was saying.

"You'll find Granville changed," Mrs. Herron told him, lining up shelf paper on the counter and marking where she wanted to cut. "Whitman's is gone—if you remember the hours we spent there." To Katie she said, "Whitman's was a school supply store. They had a soda fountain and it was a favorite gathering place after school. Before your time, of course."

She was talking just to be talking. Her voice was tense, and Katie sensed that Cousin Martin was making Mrs. Herron ill at ease. He sat at the table silently. It was hard to tell what he was thinking.

"Martin wanted to go out today, take a walk around town and see old familiar places," Mrs. Herron said to Katie. "I told him he couldn't see anything in this dreary fog."

"I could see enough," Cousin Martin said. Something about the way he said it made Katie curious about what it was he wanted to see on such a damp, foggy day. She had a feeling there was a specific place.

"And a lot of the old familiar sights aren't there anymore anyway," Mrs. Herron went on. "I drove Martin out to the shopping mall this morning—all new since he lived here. And then we drove by the new fire station. Martin always loved the old firehouse when he was a boy. He got real friendly with the firemen. They used to let him sit up on the fire engine and pretend he was driving it—when it was just there in the station, you know, and there weren't any fires going on anywhere."

Katie couldn't imagine the somber man at the kitchen table as a little boy. She wondered if he ever smiled. She also wondered why he had come for a visit after all these years.

Mrs. Herron was silent for a moment. There was only the sound of her scissors cutting the shelf paper. Then she looked at Cousin Martin with a tentative expression, as though forcing herself to speak on a subject she would rather avoid.

"Are you going to see Auntie while you're here?"

Katie peeked at Cousin Martin.

"Well, are you?" Mrs. Herron prodded.

"I might." Cousin Martin's voice was expressionless.

"I told her you were coming to visit me—" Mrs. Herron hesitated, then hurried on. "It doesn't seem right that you should be right here in town and not see her."

Cousin Martin made no answer at all, and Mrs. Herron glanced at Katie with an embarrassed look. "Our aunt—Miss Gorley," she explained. "She lives in that big old house across the street from your house."

"Miss Gorley is your aunt?" Katie was surprised.

"We're not close." Mrs. Herron shook her head quickly. "Never have been, really. But I do go over every so often to see how she is. Martin lived with her for a while when he was a little boy—after his mother died and his father took a traveling job for a time."

She paused a moment and then added, "That job didn't last, thank goodness. Martin, your father had no knack for being a salesman. He couldn't sell mittens to Eskimos."

Mrs. Herron was trying to lighten an oppressive mood that had crept into the conversation when she mentioned "Auntie." Katie felt that she was unexpectedly in the midst of private family matters, and this only made her more uncomfortable and aware of Cousin Martin's brooding presence. Mrs. Herron looked at her hopefully, but Katie couldn't think of anything to say.

Cousin Martin sat at the table, deep in his own thoughts.

He had dark hair and a small dark mustache. On his wrist a wide gold watchband showed at the cuff of his suit coat. He was rather formally dressed in a black suit and vest, and there was a stiffness about him, as though he never relaxed, never let himself laugh, never took off his coat to roll up his shirtsleeves and loosen his tie.

Maybe he was a minister, Katie thought suddenly. With his black suit and vest and his unsmiling manner he was a lot like Reverend Dean at the Methodist Church.

''It's four-thirty,'' Mrs. Herron said. She always kept track of the time. ''Martin, why don't you go in the living room and watch the early news?''

Katie was glad when Cousin Martin took this suggestion and went down the hallway toward the living room.

''Is your cousin a minister?'' she asked politely.

''A minister?'' Mrs. Herron looked up from the shelf paper with a surprised look. ''Of course not. What made you think he was a minister?''

''Oh—no reason.'' Katie felt silly for asking.

"Actually, I don't think he's employed anywhere at present." Mrs. Herron lowered her voice confidentially.

Katie thought maybe that explained why Cousin Martin had suddenly come to visit Mrs. Herron. It was a place to stay rent-free until he found a job. She watched Mrs. Herron arranging glasses on a freshly papered lower shelf. Did Mrs. Herron also think maybe her cousin had come just to have a place to stay because he was out of work?

"How long is he going to stay?" Katie asked, trying to sound nonchalant.

Mrs. Herron had finished arranging the shelf and was pouring coffee into a fresh cup. "I don't know how long Martin plans to stay. We haven't discussed it." As she went toward the kitchen doorway she added, "I'm just going to take this coffee up to John. I'll be back in a minute."

Katie was overwhelmed with disappointment. Mr. Herron was apparently upstairs in his study, as he often was in the later afternoons, and she wished she could be the one to take the coffee to him.

"I can take it," she offered, moving a step down the step stool. Mrs. Herron was already on her way. "I'll go—it's perfectly all right—I won't be a minute."

Darn! Katie thought to herself. If she hadn't been thinking so much about Cousin Martin she would have noticed Mrs. Herron getting the coffee ready: no cream, no sugar, black, the way Mr. Herron liked it—although Katie had tasted black coffee and it wasn't very good.

Cousin Martin's cup was still on the kitchen table. It looked odd to Katie, an intrusion on the quiet, orderly life of Mr. and Mrs. Herron. And she had a pretty good idea that Mrs. Herron would be glad when Cousin Martin left, even if he was her relative.

When Katie came out of the house to go home, a drizzly rain was falling. Wet leaves were pasted onto the pavement, pale yellow and limp. She hadn't seen Mr. Herron at all—which sometimes happened, but it was always a disappointment. She looked back at the house and saw the light shining in his study on the second floor.

In the living room, Cousin Martin was watching television. Katie could see him through a window where the drapes had not been drawn completely.

On Linden Street, Katie's street, the fog was moving in again as the rain grew thinner. Old Miss Gorley's house across the street from Katie's house looked more desolate than ever. It was strange to think that Cousin Martin had lived there once. A light was lit downstairs; the rest of the house, second floor and attic, towered dark in the misty rain. Katie sensed what the rooms of old-fashioned furniture and fading carpets must be like on this dreary night. She could imagine Miss Gorley sitting alone, a clock striking, shadows lurking in corners. And above, in that enormous attic at the top of the house, darkness, cupboards and closets and hiding places, nooks and crannies . . . a place where children might like to play on rainy afternoons . . . or then again, perhaps not.

Chapter Four

Cousin Martin settled into the Herron house without a word as to when he might leave.

Yet for someone settled for an indefinite stay, his room retained a bare, impersonal aspect. There were no possessions strewn around. He had brought very little with him. When Katie dusted the room she saw only one medium-size suitcase and an almost empty closet. She wondered if he had put some things into the dresser drawers, and she looked in one furtively—but it was empty. They were all empty.

To Katie there was an eeriness about the room, and she hurried to be finished there and go on to the other rooms.

Mr. Herron's study, across the hall, was definitely "lived in." Books and papers covered the big desk by the windows. There were two comfortable dark leather chairs, bookcases lined with books, and on the wall a barometer that Mrs. Herron told Katie came from an auction at an old Connecticut farmhouse. "We were there on vacation," Mrs. Herron said, as though with happy memories. "Connecticut is so beautiful—I'd like to go again."

Farther down the hall the Herrons' bedroom, although as neat and tidy as all the rest of Mrs. Herron's house, was nonetheless stamped with some marks of personality. There was often a sweater or tweed jacket of Mr. Herron's tossed across a chair. On the dressing table Mrs. Herron had carefully arranged a collection of perfume and cologne bottles, presents from birthdays and Christmases. Sachets tied with bits of ribbon were tucked into drawers and closets. In one corner there was a small desk, where Mrs. Herron kept her personalized stationery, a delicate brass swan holding letters-to-be-answered in his bill, and postage stamps in a gold lacquered box.

Downstairs in the living room, framed photographs were displayed on a table. The one Katie liked best was Mr. and Mrs. Herron's wedding picture. Mr. Herron looked solemn and very handsome. Mrs. Herron had the prettiness of a happy young girl gazing shyly from the folds of a lace wedding veil that fell gently around her face. Mrs. Herron's face was thinner now, less softly curving.

There were also photographs of Mr. Herron's

mother and father, Mrs. Herron's mother, and Mrs. Herron as a small, timid-looking girl riding a pony. Behind her on the pony a small boy was sitting.

"That's Martin," Mrs. Herron told Katie one afternoon shortly after Cousin Martin arrived. Katie looked at the picture with interest, but a straw hat shaded the boy's face and she couldn't really tell what Cousin Martin had looked like as a little boy.

Katie wondered what Cousin Martin's real home was like, wherever it was. He had come so abruptly out of nowhere. It was hard to imagine him living somewhere in a regular house or apartment, with books to read, photographs of family, the mementos and accumulations of day-by-day living.

As rootless and mysterious as he seemed to Katie, he did receive a phone call one afternoon. *He must have a friend somewhere,* she thought . . . Mrs. Herron answered the phone in the hall and went to the foot of the stairs. "Martin—telephone—" she called up to him.

In the living room a lady who had come by on some church business drew off her gloves and laid them in her lap.

Katie was watering plants by the living-room windows.

Mrs. Herron came back into the living room, lifting her eyebrows in a weary way. "My cousin is visiting us. Do you remember, I told you he was coming?"

"Yes, I remember," the church lady said. Katie

could imagine them chatting in the church foyer one Sunday morning after service.

''Out of the blue. It's been years since we've heard from him.'' Mrs. Herron shook her head. Her voice dropped, and she leaned slightly forward in her chair. Katie pretended not to be listening.

''The thing is, when will he leave?'' Mrs. Herron continued. ''It's very strange . . .'' It was hard for Katie to hear, Mrs. Herron's voice was so low.

The church lady murmured sympathetic replies. ''I had a cousin once who . . .'' But Katie couldn't hear the rest.

Before long, however, to Katie's delight, Mr. Herron arrived home.

He came into the living room, a briefcase in one hand and several books under his arm. Katie trickled water into a prayer plant, taking her time so she could stay as long as possible in the living room.

''Mrs. Linderman, nice to see you.'' Mr. Herron put down his briefcase and books. The church lady smiled at him politely.

''It's getting cold out.'' Mr. Herron rubbed his hands together. He took off his coat and laid it across the back of a chair.

''This time of year we can expect cold,'' the visiting lady said.

''We certainly can,'' Mr. Herron agreed.

There was a moment of silence, and Katie had no more plants to water.

"Hello there, Katie," Mr. Herron said, as she started out of the room.

"Hello, Mr. Herron."

There was a tall sansevieria plant in the hallway, and Katie lingered over it with the watering can . . . voices drifting to her from the living room.

"Someone phoned Martin—just a few minutes ago," Mrs. Herron said. "He's taken it on the upstairs phone. I just wonder who it could be." Then to the church lady she said, "We've no idea when he means to go. It's really rather annoying—presuming on us, after all these years."

"Oh, I understand," the church lady said sympathetically.

"Well, let's be patient." Mr. Herron's voice was lowered. Katie could barely hear the words. "Let's give him a little more time before we say anything. Things will work out."

"You don't have him on hand all day," Mrs. Herron muttered. "He gets on my nerves. Always staring out the windows."

"Always staring out the windows?" the church lady said. "At what?"

"Just staring. Very odd. Never a word about his future plans—if he has any."

The voices in the living room faded behind her as Katie went to the kitchen. She wondered if Cousin Martin had been to visit "Auntie" yet. No further mention of her had been made, at least not when Katie was around. She put the brass watering can in its place on the kitchen sill and stood for a moment gazing out across the Herrons' yard.

Who had called Cousin Martin?

Whoever it was, the call was probably over by now.

Was Cousin Martin standing silently upstairs, staring out of the guest room window at the remembered streets of his childhood? And thinking . . . thinking what?

Chapter Five

At school they began to study the New England poets in English class. Mr. Herron wrote their names on the board in his quick, short strokes. Emerson. Whittier. Bryant. Holmes. Longfellow. Lowell. He read aloud a poem of Emerson's, and Katie was so entranced just watching him that she missed the whole first verse. Mr. Herron had already paused a moment, then begun the second:

> "The foe long since in silence slept;
> Alike the conqueror silent sleeps;
> And Time the ruined bridge has swept
> Down the dark stream which seaward creeps."

Katie listened dreamily. Whatever was going on in the poem she didn't quite know; it was pleasurable enough just to listen to Mr. Herron reading aloud.

Then Mr. Herron said they could choose a poet from the names he had put on the board and write a report, due Monday.

Across the aisle, Katie saw Heather roll her eyes upward as though begging help from heaven.

"I hate 'due Monday' assignments," she told Katie after class. "They spoil the whole weekend. Let's just go to the library after school and get it over with today."

It was Thursday, so Katie was not due at the Herron house. She had, of course, told Heather all about Mrs. Herron's cousin and how he had just moved in on them, so to speak, and they didn't know how long he would stay—and they didn't really want him there. The girls had discussed all this with a secret delight in knowing something so personal and rather intimate about a teacher's home life.

"I can see why they wish he'd go," Katie had confided to Heather. "He's kind of creepy."

"How is he creepy?" Heather's blue eyes were fixed on Katie with eager curiosity.

"Just creepy. You know. He never says anything, and you never know exactly where he is. He walks around real quietly—and then suddenly there he is, watching you. But you never hear him coming. He gives me the creeps. I think he gives Mrs. Herron the creeps too. She says she never knows what he's thinking. And she looks at him in a funny way sometimes."

"What funny way?" Heather was giving Katie her complete attention.

"Well—" Katie hesitated. "It's hard to explain."

"Try," Heather urged.

"Well, like she doesn't trust him. And like maybe she's sort of afraid of him."

"Afraid of him? Her own cousin?"

Katie nodded. "Before he came, the day we were getting the guest room ready, she said no good would come of his visit. She was sort of afraid about something, even before he came."

"Wow." Heather was impressed. "This is exciting."

"I don't need the excitement." Katie laughed half-heartedly.

"They could just tell him to leave," Heather decided. "That's what I'd do."

"I suppose they could," Katie agreed. "But he *is* a relative. Anyway—what if he wouldn't leave?"

Heather frowned. "What do you mean?"

"I mean, what if they asked him and he wouldn't leave. He's weird, Heather. I told you, he's creepy."

Heather gave an exaggerated shudder. "Spooky, spooky," she whispered dramatically.

"It is sort of spooky," Katie said soberly. She remembered the feeling she had had that something bad would happen when Cousin Martin came. It hadn't happened yet—and she wished he would go away before anything really did happen.

By chance, as Katie and Heather were heading for the library after school, they saw Mr. Herron walking toward the faculty parking lot. Heather poked Katie with her elbow, to be sure Katie saw Mr. Herron. "There he is," she teased Katie with a lovesick smile.

"Very funny." Katie made a face at Heather.

Walking beside Mr. Herron was Miss Fenning, the pretty Spanish teacher, wearing a red coat and shining gold hoop earrings. Her almost black hair was ruffled becomingly by the wind, and she was laughing at something Mr. Herron had said.

Mr. Herron and Miss Fenning stopped together beside Mr. Herron's car. He opened the door on the passenger side, and Miss Fenning got in.

"He's giving her a ride home, I bet," Heather said.

Katie watched longingly as Mr. Herron got into the car. She wished she could be offered a ride home sometime. Then shyness overcame her. What would she say to Mr. Herron as they drove along? She probably wouldn't be able to think of anything to say, all alone with him. It would be terrible! Wonderful—but terrible.

As the car moved out of the parking lot, it came past Katie and Heather, and Miss Fenning waved at them through the window. She looked happy to be riding home with Mr. Herron. Very glamorous and very happy. Katie felt a pang of sympathy for Mrs. Herron and her tailored blouses and plain hair, home with her creepy cousin while Mr. Herron was offering rides to

Miss Fenning, making her laugh. It didn't seem fair somehow.

Cousin Martin had now been visiting for nearly two weeks. On Saturday afternoon Katie's mother saw him with Mrs. Herron at the shopping mall. Mrs. Allen had finished her working time at the gift shop, and was doing a few errands in the mall before going home. Mrs. Herron and Cousin Martin were just coming out of the Plants and Blooms shop, and Mrs. Herron was carefully holding a small plant swathed in thin green tissue paper. She would not trust Cousin Martin to carry it, although he had been given a few other parcels.

As the introductions were made Mrs. Herron added, "Martin, this is Katie's mother—Katie, my little helper." To Mrs. Allen she said, "Katie is such a sweet girl. I'm lucky to have her."

"Thank you." Mrs. Allen smiled. Praise for Katie always made her happy. "I've just been buying some pecan rolls for her. They're her favorite Sunday morning breakfast."

Mrs. Herron listened politely, but Cousin Martin, blinking behind his glasses, gave Katie's mother a feeling of cold hostility. She felt edgy and anxious to get away.

"It's been so nice to meet you," she said, nodding vaguely in Cousin Martin's direction as she began to move on. "Nice to see you, Mrs. Herron . . ."

At home, she found Katie in the kitchen putting peanut butter on crackers for her afternoon snack. Her father had gone on an errand to the hardware store, and Katie was alone in the house. She had on an old sweatshirt with the sleeves rolled up to her elbows, her hair tied back in a ponytail. She had been reorganizing her closet when she had suddenly felt the need for a snack.

Binky was pecking at a bit of fresh apple Katie had put between the bars of his cage. ''You need a snack too,'' she told him.

''Mom,'' she began as soon as her mother came in, ''I have nothing to wear. *Nothing*. You should see my closet. It's—''

''I know.'' Mrs. Allen nodded, repeating a well-known phrase automatically: ''It's a disaster area.''

''Yeah, it is—I'm glad you agree,'' Katie said happily. Her mother was putting packages on the table. ''Did you buy me a whole new wardrobe, maybe?''

''Not exactly. Will you settle for some pecan rolls for breakfast? By the way, I saw Mrs. Herron at the mall. And I met the cousin you told me about.''

''Isn't he weird?'' Katie moved her knife expertly around the inside of the peanut butter jar. She knew how to get the very last bit.

Mrs. Allen set down the last of her rustling packages and unbuttoned her coat. She didn't answer right away. She didn't rush to say, ''My goodness, yes, he's very weird.''

"Well, isn't he?" Katie persisted. "Isn't he weird?"

Binky fluttered in his cage, and there was the faint sound of seed scattering on the cage floor.

"Mrs. Herron's cousin is a little odd," Katie's mother admitted finally. She dropped her car keys into her purse. "I've got to call Aunt Grace tonight," she added, "about Thanksgiving."

Katie wondered if Cousin Martin would still be at the Herron house at Thanksgiving time. If he was . . . Katie tried to picture Cousin Martin sitting at the Herrons' dining-room table on Thanksgiving Day, silent, severe in his black suit and vest, turning his head to stare out of the dining-room window at nothing.

"I wouldn't be surprised if we have snow soon," Mrs. Allen said, carrying packages out of the kitchen toward the stairway.

Katie listened absently. Cousin Martin was like a shadow always at the back of her mind.

Chapter Six

"You haven't visited Auntie yet," Mrs. Herron reminded Cousin Martin.

It was Katie's Tuesday afternoon. Mrs. Herron had laid out her silver at one end of the dining-room table, to be polished. A silver tea service, serving bowls, an ornate tray, candlesticks. A heavy cloth had been spread across the part of the table where the silver was laid. Katie was polishing the candlesticks; Mrs. Herron had the teapot.

At the opposite end of the table, Cousin Martin was finishing a snack Mrs. Herron had fixed for him. Coffee and—although he had said not to bother—some crackers and slices of cheese. He sat silently, watching the silver polishing, crumbling a cracker between his fingers. Finely crushed crumbs fell to his plate like grains of sand trickling in an hourglass. It gave Katie an eerie sense of time running out.

The weather was increasingly cold now. The fog brought by the warmer days was long gone. The trees were bare and there was already a wintry bleakness to the drab yards of Bell Street where the Herron house stood.

"Auntie will be wondering why you don't come to see her," Mrs. Herron said, as she rubbed at the gleaming teapot. Her tone of voice was one of disapproval that Cousin Martin had come to town and not yet seen his very own aunt.

"I'll see her soon enough," Cousin Martin said at last, brushing bits of cracker crumbs from his fingertips. Light from the dining-room chandelier shone on his glasses, giving him a blank-eyed, mysterious look.

Katie saw Mrs. Herron's eyebrows lift, expressing a skepticism about Cousin Martin's intentions to visit Auntie.

"It's the least you can do, after all these years," she said. "The least you can do." She put the silver teapot aside and went to draw the drapes at the dining-room windows, shutting out the dark, cold afternoon and the withered lawns of Bell Street.

I'll see her soon enough, Cousin Martin had said. And this was indeed true. The very next day as Katie came home from school she saw Mrs. Herron and her cousin going up the walk to Miss Gorley's front steps.

Katie stood by her own front yard, holding her schoolbooks. Squinting a little in the cold, she watched as Mrs. Herron and Cousin Martin went up Miss Gorley's steps and stood on her porch—*the* porch, fearful scene of Halloween nights.

They rang the doorbell and stood waiting for Miss Gorley to answer.

The yard around the house was enveloped in silence. The trees stood motionless, their bare branches drawn together into the sky.

By and by Miss Gorley opened the door, and Mrs. Herron and Cousin Martin went inside the house—a house where Katie had never been, and where Laura Herron and Cousin Martin had been many times, had played as children, a house they knew well.

Katie stayed for a moment, watching the lonely house, trying to picture whatever scene was taking place inside:

Mrs. Herron sitting perhaps slightly toward the edge of her chair, as though she didn't really wish to stay long.

Cousin Martin, blinking behind his glasses, touching a finger to his dark mustache.

Old Miss Gorley, fattish, rouged, smiling sweetly. "Why haven't you been to see me sooner, Martin? Auntie is lonesome these days."

(Wasn't that what Katie's mother always said. "Poor woman all alone—here, Katie, run over to Miss Gorley's with this bread.")

But Miss Gorley was not alone this afternoon. She had her visitors. She had Mrs. Herron and Cousin Martin. Maybe she would make tea or coffee for them, Katie thought.

If Miss Gorley served any refreshments, Cousin Martin would eat in the same untasting, uninterested way he always ate, as though food were nothing to him. And Mrs. Herron would perhaps look around between bites and sips and judge the quality of the housekeeping in that great, gaunt old house that had stood on Linden Street so many years—stood when there were few other houses and only grassy meadows between, hot in summer sunlight. . . .

Finally Katie went along the side of her house to the back door and let herself in. The kitchen was wonderfully warm. Binky sang in his cage, flitting from perch to perch in joyful spirts. Katie drew off her gloves and stood by the cage, wiggling her fingers at the bars. Her cheeks were red with cold.

The bright eyes of the little bird looked at her wisely. Then he was onto another perch, trilling a song in his yellowy throat.

Katie turned as she heard steps in the hall. Her mother came along, lugging a large old clock that Katie had vague remembrances of seeing down in the basement. One of those things Dad was always promising to repair and never quite got around to.

"I'm going to see if Miss Gorley wants this clock." Mrs. Allen set the clock unceremoniously on the kitchen table and began wiping it with a cloth. "She told me once that she likes old clocks, whether they run or not, and this certainly is old and it certainly doesn't run."

"I thought Dad was going to fix it," Katie reminded her mother. They exchanged smiles above the smooth, grained surface of the clock case.

"And I want to take her some cookies." Katie's mother motioned to a plate covered with foil sitting on the counter.

"I'll help," Katie offered. "I'll take the clock and you can take the cookies."

"Sounds fair to me." Katie's mother laughed, for there was no comparing the heavy clock and the small plate of cookies.

To Katie it was a marvelous coincidence. Miss Gorley would probably invite them to come in; she'd *have* to, Katie carrying a big, heavy clock and Mrs. Allen with a plate of cookies. Then Katie could see the living room, and Mrs. Herron sitting on the edge of her chair, and Cousin Martin nibbling something . . .

But this was not to be. As Katie and her mother came out of their house, they saw Mrs. Herron and her cousin leaving Miss Gorley's house. After twenty years, Cousin Martin hadn't spent twenty minutes with "Auntie."

"Why, there're Mrs. Herron and her cousin," Katie's mother said, though Mrs. Herron did not notice them as she went on down the street.

"Miss Gorley is their aunt," Katie explained to her mother. "They sure didn't stay long. I saw them just go in a few minutes ago."

"Well, let's get over with the clock," Mrs. Allen said. "Are you sure that's not too heavy for you?"

"No, no, I'm fine," Katie insisted.

A car went by, headlights glowing in the dusk, as Katie and her mother crossed the street toward the forbidding old house. Lights were lit in only the lower windows, and the whole appearance of the house was gloomy. They stood on the porch waiting for an answer to their ring, just as Mrs. Herron and Cousin Martin had waited. A few dried leaves rustled in the corners of the porch. Silence deepened in the darkening yard.

"She must be home." Katie's mother rang the bell again—and just then Miss Gorley appeared, looming at the open door, outlined by light behind her in the hallway.

"What's this?" she said, smiling sweetly, taking in the clock and the foil-covered plate. "It's the pretty little girl. Do come in, come in . . ." And Katie was ushered into a place she had never been, laboring under the weight of the old, useless clock.

Her mother followed.

"You're always so good to me," Miss Gorley said, closing the door behind them.

The hall was less mysterious than it had looked on those Halloween nights when little Katie peeped into its shadows from the front porch. At this time of day faint light still came through narrow side windows by the door. On the landing, the round porthole window was uncurtained now and a dusky light shone on the pane.

A brass urn stood by the lower banister, and there was a small table with a mirror above, aging in a tarnished silver frame.

"You said you liked old clocks," Katie's mother said. "My husband will never get around to working on this— although he means well. I thought you might like to have it."

Miss Gorley came close to Katie and ran her fingers over the case of the clock. Her eyes had a greedy gleam.

"Yes, yes, indeed. Oh, it's lovely, lovely."

Her dress had the musty smell of closed-up rooms, and Katie drew back a step.

"Where would you like us to put the clock?" Katie's mother asked.

"We'll find a place in here, in the living room." Miss Gorley led the way. "I'd have tidied up if I'd known I was having company," she said coyly.

Katie stood in the living room holding the clock. She wanted to look around and see everything. There was a fireplace, and bookshelves on each side . . .

"Here, I think." Miss Gorley motioned to a table by the windows. She moved a glass dish of peppermint candies to make room for the clock.

Katie set the clock on the table carefully. Its hands

pointed to 8:20, as they had for all its long months in the basement at home. She felt rather sorry to see it go, after all that time.

"Candy, dearie?" Miss Gorley held the glass dish toward Katie. The peppermint candies were wrapped in cellophane. They reminded Katie of trick-or-treat candies, dropping into trick-or-treat bags, long ago.

"No, thanks," she said, shaking her head politely.

"We can't stay," Katie's mother said—although Miss Gorley had not exactly asked them to stay.

"It's a fine clock, I can see that." Miss Gorley folded her hands across her stomach and beamed at the clock. "You're too kind to a poor old woman."

"I'm glad you like it," Katie's mother said. "And these are some oatmeal cookies I baked."

Mrs. Allen had come this short distance with her coat unbuttoned, and she stood casually with her hands plunged into the coat pockets.

Katie looked around the room as fast as she could, to see everything she could before they left. She knew that any moment her mother would say, "I must get home and get dinner started."

There were no signs of cups or plates on any of the tables, so Katie guessed that no refreshments had been served to Mrs. Herron and Cousin Martin. The living-room furniture was large, with clawed feet, a dark red mahogany. The mantel was lined with a litter of objects: china dogs, brass candlesticks, seashells, small vases.

"You just had some visitors," Katie's mother said conversationally. "We saw them leaving."

Miss Gorley gestured impatiently. "I don't know what she brought him here for," she muttered. "It was just a nuisance to me."

Katie could see through a passageway to a large dining room, lost in shadows as the day ended. The table looked long, like tables large families had, with lots of people and perhaps "Auntie" at the head. The dining room seemed to echo with ghostly voices and the clatter of dishes and silverware of years gone by.

That was all Katie could see of the house—and before she had a good enough look at everything in the living room, her mother said, "Time to start dinner." She was turning toward the hall even as she spoke, and Katie followed her. Miss Gorley trailed behind, all smiles and sweetness again, crooning over the clock. "You're too kind to a poor old woman."

Outside, a few scattered flakes of snow were falling. Katie and her mother went down the steps and through Miss Gorley's silent yard.

"She didn't seem very happy about seeing her relative after twenty years," Katie said, in a low voice as though Miss Gorley might hear even behind the closed doors of her house, fading into the shadows of night.

"Families are like that sometimes," Mrs. Allen answered. "It's too bad, but it happens. Some old feud or hard feelings, perhaps."

And they let it go at that.

Chapter Seven

The snow continued falling through the night. It was not a heavy snowfall; it soon melted on the pavement where cars went by. But it clung to bushes and tree branches and window ledges. It etched rooftops in white, and drifted down on the statue of Lincoln in the town square.

Miss Gorley went to bed early, as was her custom. Her doors locked and her drapes drawn, she was closed up tight against the snowy night.

Lights burned late in Mr. Herron's study . . . but Cousin Martin's room was dark. At last, well past midnight, all the house was dark. Everyone was asleep.

By morning the snow had stopped. Katie left Binky chirping in his cage, went down the back steps and walked along to the front of the house and Linden Street.

It was the first snowfall of the year, and although it would probably melt quickly, it was special because it was the first, and for this morning at least, trees and lawns were picturesque.

As Katie reached the front of her house she stopped short with a thrill of surprise. Just entering Miss Gorley's yard across the street was Mr. Herron! His back to Katie, he went up the front walk and paused midway to the house beside a low-branched tree. He stood motionless beside the tree, his head lifted slightly to gaze up at the towering old house with its snowy roof and sills.

He didn't appear to be aware of anything but the house. And the house seemed to stare back at him, lifeless and cold, a dull, unwelcoming light streaking the windows even up to the attic story.

Feeling timid, but at the same time bold, Katie crossed the street toward Miss Gorley's house. She could just as well walk to school this way. Usually she stayed on her own side of the street until she reached the corner. Now she crossed, her heart beating faster.

What would she say to Mr. Herron?

Perhaps she could tell him she liked the New England poets.

Her mind went blank and she couldn't think of the name of even one New England poet. What if he asked her which one she liked best?

Better not to mention the New England poets.

The man by the tree didn't notice Katie coming, he was so absorbed in gazing at the silent house.

"Hello, Mr. Herron."

It took all of Katie's nerve to speak across the yard to someone so unaware of her.

The figure turned.

It was Cousin Martin.

Katie felt her face flush with embarrassment as he stared at her through his owl glasses. How could she have thought it was Mr. Herron . . . the tan overcoat, perhaps, they were so common, so many men wore overcoats just like it—and Cousin Martin's was rather like Mr. Herron's, though not exactly the same, of course.

"I'm sorry," Katie blurted out, "I thought you were Mr. Herron."

Cousin Martin was silent just long enough to increase Katie's embarrassment. "No harm done," he said at last, with a touch of—what? Contempt? A hat was pulled down close over his head, for the morning was cold, colder than it had yet been this dark November. And now that he had turned toward her, Katie could see a red muffler tucked into the neckline of the coat. It seemed like a rather bright muffler for Cousin Martin to wear, but there it was.

"Well—good-bye," Katie said awkwardly. She hurried on, feeling Cousin Martin's eyes following her until she turned the corner.

It was the last time Katie ever saw Cousin Martin.

She went on her way to school, embarrassed, disappointed, the beauty of the first snowfall forgotten. It had been so exciting to see Mr. Herron unexpectedly there so close to her own house—and it wasn't even him. She thought about what might have happened if it really had been Mr. Herron. Maybe his car was nearby—she hadn't noticed, but if it was he might have offered her a ride to school—if it really had been Mr. Herron.

More strongly than ever, Katie wished Cousin Martin would go back to wherever he had come from.

And her wish was granted.

Katie never saw Miss Gorley again either, not after that one afternoon when she was actually in Miss Gorley's house for the first and only time, there in the dim hallway and cluttered living room, putting the old clock on the table.

"Candy, dearie?" Miss Gorley, smiling, had offered peppermints.

The day after Katie saw Cousin Martin lingering in Miss Gorley's yard, Miss Gorley was found dead in an attic closet. She had been strangled with a simple bathrobe belt and carried up the narrow stairs to the attic.

Chapter Eight

Katie didn't know Miss Gorley was dead, but the day the body was found was not a "usual" day for Katie.

To begin with, Mr. Herron was not in fifth period English class. He had never before missed a class, and Katie was disappointed. Maybe he would come any moment, she thought, as time went by. The bell had already rung when finally a substitute teacher came into the room. Substitutes were usually easy to cope with, and some of the boys who didn't like English relaxed and exchanged smart looks across the aisles. Katie, of course, was sorry not to see Mr. Herron.

The next out-of-the-ordinary thing that happened was after school when Katie went to the Herron house for her regular Friday afternoon.

There was a police car in front of the Herron house.

Katie went around to the kitchen door, as she always did, glancing back at the police car as she went through the yard. What was a police car doing here? She stood at the kitchen door uncertainly, waiting for Mrs. Herron to come. But it was a policeman who opened the door for her.

"Is Mrs. Herron home?" Katie asked with some confusion. "I work for her Friday afternoons." The sight of the policeman made her feel the need to explain what she was doing at the back door, that she had a reason to be there.

"Yes, Miss, she's here," the policeman said, and Katie followed him along the hallway toward the living room.

There was an eerie quiet to the house.

Mrs. Herron was sitting in the living room, looking pale and distraught. The sight of Katie brought back the everyday world she had lost track of. "Katie! I'd forgotten all about you—oh, it's been such a day, you can't imagine."

She drew Katie toward her chair with an outstretched hand, as though seeking consolation in Katie's familiar presence.

"My aunt has been murdered, Katie," she confided in a hushed and trembling voice. "The police came to tell me this morning, when they found—when they found the body. And Cousin Martin has disappeared."

Katie stared at Mrs. Herron with amazement. Miss Gorley murdered? Cousin Martin missing? She had seen him standing in Miss Gorley's yard only yesterday morning . . .

"I phoned John at the school, after the police came, and he came right home to be with me and to make arrangements—you know, for the burial."

The burial. The words had a dreadful sound to Katie. Miss Gorley was really dead.

"We've been down at the station with the police, and now they're here to see if they can find anything in Martin's room that will be helpful in finding him."

Mrs. Herron paused, distressed. Her face showed signs of fatigue and strain.

"They think perhaps—perhaps it might have been Martin who killed Auntie."

"Your cousin Martin?" Katie was trying to take in what Mrs. Herron was saying, but it was all too unbelievable. "They think *he* killed Miss Gorley."

"Yes—and they may be right." Mrs. Herron lifted her hands helplessly. "Oh, Katie, it's been such a terrible day."

"When did he disappear?" Katie was still trying to understand.

"Yesterday afternoon. I was out for a while, and when I came home he was gone."

Katie could see that the policeman, standing nearby, was listening too, and Mrs. Herron began to talk to him now, as well as to Katie.

"At first we thought 'good riddance.' We were just glad he was gone, even though it was odd he'd leave without a word. Then this morning when they found Auntie, well, it made things look different. Suspicious.''

Voices in the hall distracted Mrs. Herron, and she turned in her chair. Katie, too, looked toward the hall; Mr. Herron and another man were coming down the stairs. The man wore a plain gray suit and coat, but Katie guessed at once that he was a policeman.

''Did you find anything?'' Mrs. Herron asked anxiously, as the two men came into the living room.

''Nothing very helpful, I'm afraid,'' the plainclothesman answered, shaking his head.

Coming behind him, Mr. Herron noticed Katie and nodded. ''Hello, Katie.''

''Katie comes and helps me on Friday afternoons,'' Mrs. Herron explained to the man in the gray coat. ''I forgot she was coming today—I've been so upset. Katie, this is Detective Brant.''

The police detective looked at Katie with interest. ''You come here every Friday?'' he inquired.

Katie nodded.

''And Tuesdays,'' Mrs. Herron added.

''Is that so? Then you know this Martin Gorley? Met him when you came here those afternoons?''

''Yes.'' Katie nodded again.

''Katie hardly saw much of him,'' Mrs. Herron said.

Detective Brant acknowledged this with a courteous nod. ''Nevertheless, she might know something, some little thing that will help.''

He was a small man, balding, rather kindly-looking. He put Katie as much at ease as she could be under the circumstances. Her mind was still spinning with all Mrs. Herron had told her.

"Did you ever hear him say anything that would give you any idea of his hometown, where he came from, what type of work he did?"

Katie shook her head.

"Did you ever go into his room upstairs?"

"I dusted there," Katie said.

"Did you ever see anything there that gave you any idea where he might be from—or anything that seemed unusual in any way?"

Again Katie shook her head. Cousin Martin's room had always been so bare, so impersonal. It was as though he had purposely meant to leave no clue or trace of himself when he was gone. She remembered the solitary suitcase, the empty bureau drawers. It would be easy for him to take everything away in the wink of an eye, there was so little to take.

"I did see him at Miss Gorley's house yesterday morning," Katie added timidly, "on my way to school."

The tension in the room grew. Katie could feel it tightening around her. She had seen Cousin Martin at Miss Gorley's house . . . and now Miss Gorley was dead.

Detective Brant regarded her intently. "What time would that have been?"

"About eight-thirty."

"Did you speak to him?"

"I said hello, because at first I thought it was Mr. Herron. He was standing in the yard, just looking at the house. But it was Cousin Martin."

"Did you actually see him go into the house?"

"No, I didn't. I had to go on to school. He was still standing there when I got to the corner. I looked back then, and I could see him. His red muffler was easy to see."

"A red muffler." Detective Brant smiled wryly. "Yes, that would be easy to spot. And standing for a period of time in the yard, before going in—presuming he did eventually go in. It's almost like he *wanted* to be seen there, to be noticed and remembered."

The room was silent as Detective Brant let his words rest. Katie glanced at Mr. Herron. He had moved across the room to stand by the table where the framed family photographs were displayed. She knew he had been listening to what she said. Having his attention on her made her even more self-conscious.

"Perhaps Martin just wanted to see Auntie," Mrs. Herron said hesitantly. "It doesn't mean he killed her."

"No, of course not," the detective agreed calmly, "but you have already told me that he didn't get on with his aunt, and didn't even go to see her for some time after he was in town, despite your urging. It seems odd that he would then go off on a second social call all on his own."

"Yes—I suppose it would be," Mrs. Herron agreed faintly.

"I believe this is the only photograph we have of Martin," Mr. Herron said from his side of the room. He took up the snapshot of Mrs. Herron riding the pony with the small boy behind her. "No good to you, I'm afraid."

Detective Brant took the picture and studied it briefly. "No, not much use," he agreed reluctantly. He handed the picture back to Mr. Herron. "I have an idea this fellow may not be easy to find. You've described him with glasses and a mustache. Those things completely change a person. If, as you say, you hadn't seen him for twenty years, he could easily disguise his looks a bit and all the more easily vanish when the murder was done. And at the moment, it does seem as if he came here with that purpose: murder."

"I can't believe he could do such a thing," Mrs. Herron said.

"No one answering his description was seen on any of the buses leaving town yesterday." Detective Brant continued his train of thought. "He may look entirely different now. We have to consider every angle."

He turned to Mrs. Herron.

"You said that your cousin came back here from what he told you was simply a morning walk—a walk which we now know from this young lady"—he nodded to Katie—"was to Miss Gorley's house. Then he went to his room complaining of a headache."

"That's right," Mrs. Herron said. "I went out to do some shopping in the early afternoon. He was still in his room when I left. I was only gone for about an hour, and when I came back I went upstairs to see if he felt better and wanted something to eat. But he was gone. Everything was gone." She gestured with bewilderment. "Everything. Gone. He had just vanished."

"It all seems pretty obvious," Mr. Herron said, "and very carefully planned."

"Yes, very carefully planned," Detective Brant repeated, almost to himself. "And yet, there's something odd . . ." He shook his head, as if exasperated that he could not say exactly what it was that was odd.

Katie sensed that the interview was drawing to an end. The detective held his hat in his hand in the manner of someone about to put it on and leave. The uniformed policeman, still standing at the side of the room attentively, also looked like he was about to leave.

"We'll have this house fingerprinted, as well as the Gorley house," Detective Brant concluded, "but I doubt we'll come up with anything. Your cousin brought few things, as you've told me, so he was prepared for a quick getaway. Someone planning everything so carefully isn't likely to go off leaving a nice set of prints for us to find."

"No, I suppose not," Mr. Herron said regretfully.

"The inquest will be some day next week." Detective Brant turned to Katie one last time. "You'll probably be called to give your testimony, Katie. You worked in the house here, and you actually saw this man at the Gorley house on the day of the murder.''

Katie felt a sense of misgiving. To give testimony at an inquest sounded like such a responsibility. And what if Cousin Martin came back to get even with her for saying she saw him? Katie didn't even want to think about that.

''Oh, you must find him,'' Mrs. Herron said with an urgent tone as she saw the policemen preparing to go. ''Poor Auntie. You *must* find him.''

''We'll do our best,'' the police detective promised.

And a search was launched for Cousin Martin—who had disappeared like a puff of wind into the air.

Chapter Nine

Now here was something unusual and highly sensational to be reported in *The Granville News*—the only murder story ever printed in those pages.

The aura of murder hung over the small, peaceful town, a cloud darker than those of the November skies above.

No one in Granville had ever before been murdered in cold blood. It was the subject of conversation in every house along the quiet, tree-lined streets. Cars of curious onlookers crept along Linden Street at a snail's pace while drivers and passengers gaped at the house. Other people came on foot, and stood about staring at the house where the body had been found in an attic closet.

When Katie came downstairs for breakfast Saturday morning, her father was standing at the living-room bay window, watching the slow-going cars and the people lingering along the edge of Miss Gorley's yard. His handsome dark eyes were clouded with concern.

"Who would ever have thought something like this would happen?" he said to Katie as she came to stand in the circle of his arm. "A murder right here, across the street from our house."

Together they went back to the kitchen, and Katie's father tried to make the morning less somber. "Ah, Katie, no one makes coffee like your mother," he said with a rather forced air of cheerfulness.

"You're just saying that because it's true," Katie's mother answered modestly.

And Binky was singing in his cage.

But it just wasn't the usual Saturday morning. A murder right across the street was not something quickly forgotten.

Heather came to spend Saturday afternoon at Katie's house. *The Granville News* had come and they spread the newspaper on the floor in Katie's room and hung over it, absorbing every detail with incredulous gasps and shivers.

They found out how the body had actually been discovered.

The newspaper account said:

Miss Gorley's next-door neighbor, Mrs. Merriman, had made arrangements earlier in the week to take Miss Gorley grocery shopping Friday morning. Mrs. Merriman did this every so often, as a neighborly gesture. Miss Gorley had no car of her own.

On Friday morning, at the appointed time, Mrs. Merriman phoned Miss Gorley to see if she was ready. Miss Gorley did not answer her phone. Mrs. Merriman tried again a few minutes later, and when Miss Gorley still did not answer, Mrs. Merriman went over to the house and rang Miss Gorley's doorbell. She knew Miss Gorley looked forward to these shopping trips and would not miss one.

When Miss Gorley did not answer the doorbell, Mrs. Merriman returned to her own home and phoned the police. Her fear was that Miss Gorley had been taken ill, or fallen in the house.

"Just think"—Heather hugged herself and shivered dramatically—"there Miss Gorley was all the time, stuffed in the closet."

It was a horrible thing to think about.

The newspaper report continued:

Miss Gorley's nephew, Martin Gorley, had been visiting his cousin, Laura Herron (wife of John Herron, faculty member at Granville High School). Mr. Gorley was not on good terms with his aunt, and had been only occasionally in touch with members of his family since he left Granville twenty years ago.

The sudden and mysterious disappearance of Martin Gorley the day of the murder points a strong finger of suspicion.

The police feel that finding him may be a challenge. They speculate that he may have come to Granville disguised by glasses and a mustache, the removal of which disguise would facilitate his disappearance.

Mrs. Herron has stated that when her cousin came to visit her he said little about himself. She does not know where he last lived, and she has no idea at all as to where he might have gone.

''How will they ever find him?'' Katie moaned.

''Maybe they never will,'' Heather said darkly. ''I bet lots of murderers are never caught.''

They read on curiously.

However Mrs. Herron, niece of the murdered woman, was able to shed some light on the choice of the attic closet as a place for the murder victim.

''When we were children,'' Mrs. Herron said, ''Martin was sometimes naughty. At least our aunt thought he was naughty. She would lock him in a closet in her attic, as punishment.''

''How awful.'' Katie made a face. ''What a terrible thing to do.''

"And he never forgot it," Heather added ominously.

"No." Katie considered this with awe. "After all these years, he never forgot it."

How terrified and panicky a child must feel to remember something so intently and to want such a revenge so many years later.

Katie was sure now that it was "Auntie's" house that Cousin Martin had wanted to see that day it was so foggy. *Martin wanted to go out today, take a walk around town and see old familiar places,* Mrs. Herron had said. *I told him he couldn't see anything in this dreary fog.*

I could see enough, Cousin Martin had said.

It was "Auntie's" house he had wanted to see.

And then he had stood so strangely in the yard that morning Katie had seen him last, just staring at the house, up toward the attic . . . remembering. After all these years.

The newspaper story concluded with the information that Miss Gorley had been a citizen of Granville for eighty years. Services were to be private.

When Heather had gone home, Katie wandered downstairs and stood by the living-room window, looking at the house across the street. There were still a few slow cars going by, still a few people standing on the sidewalk in front of the house. It was nearing twilight.

The house looked grim and frightening to Katie. She tried to picture it years ago, on sunshiny summer days when children had played in the yard, run up and down the porch steps. Maybe once there had been a porch swing.

Katie couldn't picture Miss Gorley as younger, or in any way different than the elderly woman she had always known.

Nor could she picture Cousin Martin as a child. As a child, he was only a vague figure in a photograph, a small boy on a pony. She was glad he was gone from the Herron house. He had made her uneasy, appearing suddenly and silently around the turn of a doorway, watching her from behind the thick lenses of his glasses. Had he really needed those glasses? Or was he perhaps disguised, as Detective Brant had suggested? *We have to consider every angle,* he had said.

The house across the street was dark.

Even when Katie came away from the window, the memory of that dark house stayed in her mind.

Chapter Ten

Sunday, the curiosity seekers came again, though fewer now. A cold rain drizzled down at intervals. Passing cars had windshield wipers turned on. Pedestrians came with umbrellas, or jacket hoods drawn up around their heads.

It was a long, dreary day for Katie. Her mother proceeded with Thanksgiving preparations to the extent of asking Katie's father to get the turkey platter down from a high cupboard shelf. It was a tremendous platter, kept on the highest shelf because it was so rarely used.

Katie's father did this during halftime of a football game he was watching on television.

"There," Mrs. Allen said with satisfaction, when the platter was down from the shelf and placed on a kitchen counter, "isn't that a wonderful platter?"

"It's a *heavy* platter," Katie's father said, as though this was honor enough. Then he went back to the football game.

Katie carried the platter to the dining-room buffet, where other special things for Thanksgiving Day had begun to accumulate. The special water goblets her mother used only for company. Two ceramic pilgrims about four inches high that had been on every Thanksgiving table since Katie could remember. A wicker cornucopia that would be filled with nuts and apples and ears of dried corn for the Thanksgiving dinner centerpiece. Aunt Grace was coming, of course, and Grandma and Grandpa Allen, aunts and uncles and small children.

As the day dragged on, Katie thought with mixed feelings about the inquest to come.

It would probably be exciting. There was no question about that.

She might never go to another inquest in her whole entire life.

Kids at school would envy her. They all knew about the murder, but *she* was the only one going to the inquest. It made her feel important.

Still, she went to bed Sunday night dreading the inquest.

They would ask her about Cousin Martin.

She remembered the first time she had ever met him. He was sitting at Mrs. Herron's kitchen table, drinking coffee. Mrs. Herron was cutting strips of shelf paper. Cousin Martin was stirring sugar into his coffee.

Are you going to see Auntie while you're here? Mrs. Herron had asked.

I might, Cousin Martin had said.

Katie fell asleep at last, dreaming that Cousin Martin was watching her—from wherever he was.

Monday after school Katie went to Heather's house to make fudge.

"My mom's got a new recipe you won't believe," Heather promised.

Heather lived on Poplar Street, a street well named, lined with giant poplars. A rustic redwood fence surrounded the large yard; redwood boxes banded with brass were empty of flowers now, beside the front steps of the house.

The girls sat in Heather's kitchen, watching the pan of bubbling chocolate. Heather's silver earrings glittered in the light as she moved her head. From somewhere else in the house Katie could hear Heather's mother laughing as she played with Heather's little brother. It was a nice, comforting sound. And the warm chocolaty pan on the stove was comforting too. But the inquest was still heavy on Katie's mind.

"Oh, Heather—I just don't want to go to the inquest," she said at last. She slumped at the kitchen table, looking to Heather for sympathy.

"It's exciting." Heather turned from the bubbling pan of fudge, her spoon lifted. "Aren't you excited?"

"Well, sort of," Katie admitted grudgingly. "I

think I'd like to just go to the inquest and see it, and not have to answer questions.''

''Oh, no, no, no.'' Heather waved her fudge spoon. ''The inquest will be exciting!''

Katie sighed. ''It's exciting to you because you don't have to do it.''

''I wish I could,'' Heather said eagerly. She left the stove and came to sit by Katie at the kitchen table. ''And you know what I've been thinking,'' she added, lowering her voice.

''What?'' Katie looked at Heather curiously.

''I've been thinking about what it said in the newspaper—about how the police say it might be hard to find that man. They think it might be hard to find him because maybe he was disguised, and no one like him was seen leaving town. But what if he hasn't left town?''

''What do you mean?'' Katie stared across the table at Heather.

''I mean, what if he's still right here in town?''

Katie thought about that with a feeling of confusion. ''Why would he still be here?'' she asked.

''That would be a really neat way to hide, wouldn't it?'' Heather leaned across the table. ''Maybe he never even left town at all. It's the last place anyone would look for him. He'd be safe here.''

''You mean he could still be here in Granville?'' Katie didn't find the idea of Cousin Martin still being in town a very cheerful idea.

"Sure he could still be here," Heather said. She got up to check the fudge. "He could be right here in town this very minute. What better way to hide?"

Katie started home from Heather's house about five o'clock. The afternoons were shorter than ever now, and colder, she thought, as she snuggled her chin into the knit scarf wrapped around her neck. Her mother had knit the scarf; the long fringe swung gracefully as Katie walked along toward Linden Street.

It was almost completely dark. The last leaves were gone from the trees.

Then, just as she turned down Linden Street, Katie had a sense of uneasiness. She turned to look behind her, but the street was deserted. She paused and then walked on, glancing back now and then. Even deserted, the street had an ominous look. *Was* there someone there behind her, lost from sight in the darkness, slipping behind a tree to hide?

She began to walk more quickly. In the block ahead she could see Miss Gorley's house against the twilight sky. And across the street was her own house. She would be home soon . . . and she wanted to be home, to be safely home. No one was following her, of course; it was just the dark, silent street and the recent murder that were making her jumpy . . . and what Heather had said about Cousin Martin still being in town.

Katie looked back again at the empty street. No one

was there. Light from a streetlamp was shining on the pavement . . . a car went by . . . the street was quiet again . . . deserted.

Katie reached her house with relief. The yard was in deep darkness. No lights shone at the windows. Monday was one of her mother's days at the gift shop.

Katie hurried through the yard and up the front steps. She tried the door. Sometimes Mom forgot to lock up. But not this time. Not this door. It was securely locked.

Katie opened her shoulder-strap bag and got out her key. All around her the yard and trees and shadows lay in a mysterious night-silence.

The dark silence seemed to breathe.

Almost as though someone was there.

Some real person.

A car went by. Then another car. There were lights on in the house next door. A faint sound of piano music drifted out into the evening.

Katie turned her key in the lock, opened the door, and stood safe at last in her own entryway.

She turned on the hall light—and then on an impulse, went down the hallway toward the kitchen. Her mother forgot to lock the kitchen door too, sometimes, and Katie didn't want any unlocked doors tonight. She wanted to feel safe, this dark November night.

"Hi, Binky."

As Katie turned on the kitchen light, the little bird scurried up to a perch. Light gleamed on the windowpanes. A bowl of nuts and ears of corn, for the Thanksgiving cornucopia, were on the kitchen table.

Katie went toward the door—but she was too late.

As she went toward it, the door burst open suddenly.

Someone stood there, face hidden by a Frankenstein-monster mask.

There was hardly time to scream as Katie drew back from the frightening masked face at the door. She turned and fled almost the same moment that the door burst open—knocking against the kitchen table and sending the nuts and ears of corn scattering across the kitchen floor.

She ran through the dark house toward the front door, her heart bursting, pounding with fear.

Chapter Eleven

Katie was in a nightmare. Nothing was real.

As she half-stumbled, half-ran down her front steps and through her yard toward the street, nothing was real.

Across the street Miss Gorley's house stood forsaken beyond the circle of light cast by the streetlamp.

Other houses along the street blurred in Katie's sight . . . just houses . . . lighted windows . . . dark yards.

Headlights of passing cars.

A mailbox at the corner.

A dog in a yard, barking as she ran by.

She heard no pursuing footsteps behind her, but she ran headlong, goaded by fear.

The sight of that masked face lunging at her through the kitchen door would never be forgotten.

Where was she running—?

Nowhere.

Only *away*.

And then, gasping for breath at the intersection of Linden and Maple Streets—three blocks from home!—Katie was aware of a car slowing to a stop.

The car window was rolled down, and a dear, familiar voice called, ''Katie? Hi, there.''

Her mother's voice had never sounded so good. Tears sprang into Katie's eyes then, the tears of fright and panic she had been too stunned to shed in her wild flight from the house.

''Mom—Mom—'' Katie went toward the car, seeing everything vaguely through a blur of tears.

''Katie—what is it?''

Katie heard the sudden concern in her mother's voice.

''Mom—there's someone at the house—''

Katie yanked open the car door hysterically. She was shaking as she got in, and a flood of tears burst loose. ''Oh—Mom—Mom—it was awful—''

She felt her mother's arms around her.

''It's all right, honey—it's all right. Now calm down.''

A passing car honked impatiently and then went around Mrs. Allen's car, stopped at the intersection.

''Don't cry, honey,'' the soothing voice pleaded. ''Tell me what happened.''

''Someone was there,'' Katie sobbed, ''he came in the kitchen door with this mask—oh, Mom, I never want to go back there—''

* * *

Mrs. Allen drove at once to the Granville police station. It was a small red brick building across the square from the town hall. A single squad car was parked in front, under the bright rays of the streetlamp.

Mrs. Allen, fresh from the innocent concerns of the gift shop, sat somewhat flustered on the corridor bench to which she and Katie were directed.

"Sergeant Wells will be with you in a minute," a young policewoman said.

Katie sat stiffly beside her mother, feeling a unique sense of tension at actually being in the police department building.

Somewhere in offices farther down the corridor, a phone was ringing. Katie could hear it, muted behind closed doors.

Katie's mother stood up with restless relief when Sergeant Wells appeared and said, "This way, please." She put her arm protectively around Katie's shoulders, there in the bleak light of the police station hallway.

"Everything's going to be all right," she whispered to Katie as they walked into the small room Sergeant Wells led them to.

There were filing cabinets against one wall. Sergeant Wells sat behind a gray metal desk. It was the most cheerless place Katie had ever seen . . . but it was a safe place . . . she felt the safeness of it . . . no one could hurt her here.

"My daughter—" Mrs. Allen began.

Sergeant Wells lifted a hand. "Let her tell it," he said.

So, trembling, Katie told how she had been walking home from Heather's house and had a feeling of being followed.

"Did you actually see anyone following you?" Sergeant Wells asked. He was a solemn, dark-eyed man; he seemed weary of sad stories.

"No, I didn't *see* anybody, but somebody was there—I know somebody was there."

Tears had dried on Katie's cheeks. She felt unlike herself: grubby somehow, shy, stared at, miserable. She was in a strange place.

"When I got in the house, I went to the kitchen to be sure the door was locked."

She glanced at her mother.

"Just as I got there, the door came open—and—and—someone was there—someone awful—coming at me—"

The office was silent.

Mrs. Allen moved slightly in her chair and reached out to pat Katie's arm.

"Then what happened?" she asked softly.

Sergeant Wells waited without speaking.

Katie took a deep breath. "Well—then—I just ran."

As she spoke she could hear the sound of the bowl of nuts and ears of corn crashing to the kitchen floor.

"Mom—all your stuff fell off the table, your

Thanksgiving stuff.'' Katie was almost apologetic. ''I think he stumbled on it—''

''And you were able to get away.'' Sergeant Wells tapped a pencil on his gray metal desk.

Katie shrank into her chair, feeling the fright of the moment sweep over her again. Remembering the hideous masked figure lunging at her through the kitchen door.

''I guess that's how I got away,'' she whispered. It could only have been a moment that the masked person stumbled on the scattered nuts and ears of corn. But it had been enough. It had given Katie the moment she needed to escape.

The clock on the office wall pointed to 5:46. The hand moved forward with a jerking motion, and it was 5:47.

It was almost time for Katie's father to come home from work.

''We'll send a squad car over to check your house,'' Sergeant Wells said. ''However, I'm sure the intruder is gone by now.''

The phone on the desk rang, and Sergeant Wells answered it. ''Not tonight—tell Anderson to cover it.''

Routine police work was going on.

Katie stared down at her own clasped hands.

''Can you tell us anything more?'' the police sergeant asked.

Katie hesitated. She wanted to be sure . . . but she *was* sure. She *was*.

"The Frankenstein mask he had on had a rip in the chin. I saw it before, at Mrs. Herron's house. In a box of costumes she had in her basement."

There was a long moment—and then Katie's mother said fearfully, "At Mrs. Herron's house? Then he's come back. Her cousin Martin has come back."

Detective Brant was summoned to the office where Katie and her mother were sitting.

"I think you'll be interested in this," Sergeant Wells told him. "Someone broke into this girl's house a short time ago—someone she thinks might be Martin Gorley."

"Martin Gorley?" Detective Brant's eyes narrowed. He leaned toward Katie with an intent expression. "Why would he wish to harm you?"

Katie stared back fearfully. She felt shaky again, not like herself at all.

Why would Cousin Martin want to harm her? Because she had seen him standing in Miss Gorley's yard? His disappearance from town was more incriminating than Katie seeing him in the yard.

"Why would Martin Gorley wish to harm you?" Detective Brant repeated.

Katie's mother looked at her with bewilderment.

"I don't know," Katie said. Tears glistened in her eyes and slid down her cheeks. "I don't know—he was just there all of a sudden—"

The awful memory came back. The kitchen door

bursting open, the Frankenstein mask, the figure lunging toward her.

"Why would he still be here in town?" Detective Brant asked himself. He didn't expect an answer from anyone in the room.

He lapsed into silence, absorbed in thought.

The police sergeant waited without comment. Katie felt her mother's reassuring hand on her arm.

"I think it would be a good idea to go to the Herron house and let them know about this development," Detective Brant said at last. "Let's see if it makes any sense to them. It doesn't make much sense to me."

Chapter Twelve

The night had grown sharply colder. The sky was clear and densely black above the leafless trees. Later there would be a moon.

At the Herron house, lights shone from the living-room windows, casting squares of pale light on the darkened yard.

The house looked cheerful and cozy, with its lights shining out into the night.

Katie got out of the police car and walked with her mother and Detective Brant toward the front door.

She had always gone to the kitchen door when she came on Tuesday and Friday afternoons. . . . She remembered the afternoon Cousin Martin had been sitting at the kitchen table when she came.

Now she was going to the front door.

The same uniformed policeman who had been with Detective Brant before, followed Katie, her mother, and Detective Brant along the Herrons' front walk.

Mrs. Herron answered the bell with an expression of surprise to see Katie and her mother and the police standing there.

"We're sorry to disturb you," Detective Brant said in his courteous way. "Something has come up that I think will be of interest to you. May we come in?"

"Yes, of course." Mrs. Herron stepped back, holding the door open more widely.

Katie could see Mr. Herron coming from the living room to see what was going on.

They stood in the living room in a rather awkward group.

"Please—sit down." Mrs. Herron gestured toward the sofa. She looked particularly at Katie and her mother, as though she thought perhaps the policemen would not want to sit, being on business.

"Thank you," Katie's mother said. She sat in a chair by the sofa and held her handbag in her lap. Katie sat on the edge of a sofa cushion. Detective Brant and the policeman remained standing. The room around them was in perfect order, as always. Magazines on the coffee table lay overlapping one another in an orderly row. Mrs. Herron had been drinking a cup of tea, and the cup, half empty, was on a table at the end of the sofa. The room seemed overly warm after the cold of the night.

"We think that perhaps Martin Gorley may still be here in Granville," Detective Brant began.

"Here in town?" Mrs. Herron stared at Detective Brant with complete amazement. "But he's gone—he disappeared."

"Perhaps not," Detective Brant said.

Mr. Herron stepped forward, frowning. "What are you saying? Have you seen Martin?"

Detective Brant turned toward Mr. Herron, shaking his head. "No, I haven't seen him, but just a short while ago this young lady was surprised in her home by someone wearing a Frankenstein mask. A mask she remembers seeing in this house."

Mrs. Herron looked at Katie blankly. "In this house. I don't understand."

"Neither do I," Mr. Herron said.

"I saw it downstairs, in the basement, when you were putting the costumes away after the Halloween party. It was in the trunk."

Katie felt all eyes upon her as she turned to Mrs. Herron.

"Don't you remember? You were putting away the Romeo and Juliet costumes from the party."

"I don't understand." Mrs. Herron looked from Katie to Detective Brant with an expression of confusion. "What would that have to do with Martin?"

Almost before she realized it, Katie heard herself saying, ''No, it wouldn't have anything to do with him.''

Detective Brant swung around and fixed her with a piercing gaze.

''Katie—'' Mrs. Allen said anxiously, ''it must have been Cousin Martin wearing the mask—''

''No. No.'' Katie shook her head furiously. ''Cousin Martin wasn't even here then!''

A clear memory of the afternoon was coming back to her. She and Mrs. Herron had put the Halloween things in the trunk, and Mr. Herron had moved all the Christmas boxes in front of the trunk. . . . Then she had gone upstairs with Mrs. Herron to get the guest room ready for Cousin Martin . . . *No good will come of this visit,* Mrs. Herron had said.

Cousin Martin didn't come until *after* the Halloween things had been stored away behind the Christmas decorations. He wouldn't even know the trunk of costumes was there—and he certainly wouldn't just accidentally come across a Halloween mask packed away in the basement behind big cardboard boxes of Christmas stuff.

Katie looked up and met the thoughtful eyes of Detective Brant.

''Martin Gorley wasn't here when the Halloween things were put away?'' he asked.

Katie shook her head. ''He didn't come until the next day. We were getting the room ready for him.''

Detective Brant was silent for a moment. He was thinking the same things Katie was thinking, asking himself the same questions. Katie's mother moved uneasily in her chair, glancing at Mrs. Herron.

"Katie," Detective Brant began slowly, "did you ever see Martin Gorley with Mr. Herron?"

It was an odd question, and Katie was taken by surprise. She tried to think back over the past weeks . . . Cousin Martin drinking coffee at the kitchen table, watching television in the living room, eating his snack while Katie polished silver at the dining-room table, appearing around doorways when she least expected him, going with Mrs. Herron to visit Miss Gorley, standing alone that last snowy morning in Miss Gorley's yard.

"No, I guess not," Katie answered hesitantly, looking quickly over toward Mr. Herron. She never had seen them together, now that she thought of it.

The silence in the room grew ominous.

"I suggest," Detective Brant said, "that the reason you never saw Mr. Herron and Martin Gorley at the same time, together, is because Mr. Herron and Martin Gorley were the same person. In other words, there really was no Martin Gorley."

Katie stared at Detective Brant.

"But—but—he had a telephone call—"

"Did you see him answering the phone?"

"Well, no," Katie admitted. "He took the call on the upstairs phone."

"A call made by Mr. Herron on his way home from school." Detective Brant moved his attention to Katie's mother. "And you, Mrs. Allen, where did you meet this Cousin Martin?"

"Out at the shopping mall one Saturday," Katie's mother said faintly.

"Yes, Saturday, when there is no school. Of course. And he was with Mrs. Herron?"

"Yes."

"Not Mr. Herron? Only Mrs. Herron?"

"Yes, with Mrs. Herron."

Detective Brant nodded with satisfaction. "Mrs. Herron talked about her cousin—to Katie and no doubt to neighbors and friends. She took him around town shopping with her so that people would see him. But I think if people in town were questioned, no one would actually remember a Martin Gorley living here twenty years ago. And who would bother checking old school records or birth records to see if there ever really was such a person?"

Detective Brant faced Mr. Herron across the living room.

"You, Mr. Herron, were Martin Gorley. You had knowledge of the Halloween masks in the basement, and could easily get one when you needed it. It was your bad luck you chose one Katie had seen."

Everyone turned toward Mr. Herron, who stood as motionless as a figure carved from stone.

"And you needed the mask to kill Katie."

Katie's mother gasped. Her hands flew to her face as if to shield herself from these dreadful words.

Mrs. Herron's forehead was furrowed with confusion. She looked toward her husband for comfort that wasn't there. Mr. Herron's face was taut and expressionless.

"Why—" Mrs. Herron asked in a trembling voice, "why would you harm Katie?"

Mr. Herron did not answer.

"Katie thought it was Mr. Herron she saw standing in Miss Gorley's yard," Detective Brant said. "When she told us that, I thought it was odd. Why would she think it was Mr. Herron? She saw some similarity of movement as he walked, perhaps, a gesture, a turn of the head." Detective Brant shrugged. "She saw something that surpassed the disguise of dark hair, mustache, glasses. She knew Mr. Herron when she saw him."

So many classroom hours Katie had watched Mr. Herron at his desk, walking to the blackboard, standing by the windows, gesturing, strolling down an aisle. There was his own way of moving that she knew, without ever having to see his face.

"Yes, Katie recognized you, Mr. Herron." Detective Brant faced the English teacher. "I think you were afraid that at the inquest she would repeat what she told me, that at first she thought it was you standing in Miss Gorley's yard. You were afraid that somehow *someone* would eventually put two and two together."

Detective Brant paused.

"As I have done."

No one spoke.

"Of course your wife was part of the 'Cousin Martin' plot," Brant continued, "but I don't think she knew anything about what happened this afternoon, the threat to Katie's life."

A muffled cry drew Katie's attention to Mrs. Herron. She shrank in her chair, looking more like the dark-eyed timid girl in the photo, the little girl on the pony—with some forgotten neighbor child of long ago. An expression of acute distress filled her dark eyes now, as she looked at her husband with disbelief that he could have really wanted to kill Katie.

Then, defeated, drained of all attempts at deception, Mrs. Herron spoke with anguish.

"Yes, I agreed to the Cousin Martin disguise—we needed the money she was going to leave me—John wanted to travel—he said he felt trapped here in Granville—he never really liked teaching—"

"Shut up, Laura." Mr. Herron spit out the words with fury.

"—but she never died—all the years were going by, and we wanted the money—we *needed* it—"

Mrs. Herron looked around the room desperately. Even she knew how contemptible her confession sounded.

"I didn't really care about the money," she sobbed. "I hated Auntie. I wanted her to die. I was the one locked in the attic. I was the one."

Chapter Thirteen

There never really had been a Cousin Martin.

All the conversations about him to Katie and neighbors, how unexpected his visit was, how long it would last, intimations that no good would come of it, had all been thoughtfully planned to create the reality of someone named Martin Gorley who had once lived in Granville and had now returned—to murder his aunt.

Mrs. Herron had made up a fake name for ''Cousin Martin'' when she took him to visit Miss Gorley. No wonder Miss Gorley had showed no interest in him. *I don't know what she brought him here for,* she said. *It was just a nuisance to me.*

Now Miss Gorley was gone, after eighty years in Granville.

On the afternoon of the murder, Mr. Herron had calmly taught his classes at the high school, while Mrs. Herron had driven out into the countryside and disposed of the "Cousin Martin" suitcase, the black suit, wig, mustache, and eyeglasses.

Miss Gorley had more money than anyone suspected. As her only living relative, Mrs. Herron would have had it all. The money, plus what would come from the sale of the house and furnishings. A considerable amount—although, serving prison terms, the Herrons would do no traveling with the money.

For long after, Katie had bad dreams of Mr. Herron lunging through the kitchen door. She had had a crush on him—and one dark November afternoon he had tried to kill her.

Katie and Heather talked about the Herrons sometimes, remembering how Mr. Herron had walked with Miss Fenning through the faculty parking lot. Pretty Miss Fenning with her red coat and black wind-tousled hair. How often did he drive her home like that? they wondered. She had laughed at what Mr. Herron was saying.

"Maybe Mrs. Herron thought if she inherited all that money, Mr. Herron would love her more," Heather said once.

"I don't know," Katie said.

She had a sad feeling when she thought about Mrs. Herron.

Everything in her house was so neat and tidy.

A bowl of wax fruit sat on the exact center of the dining-room buffet.

Magazines were arranged just so on the coffee table.

There was fresh shelf paper on her kitchen shelves.

But once upon a time, Mrs. Herron had been a little girl, terrified in a locked closet on a suffocating summer day.

And she had remembered it all the years after.

It was only Auntie's little joke . . .